Close at Heart
A Sea Otter Story

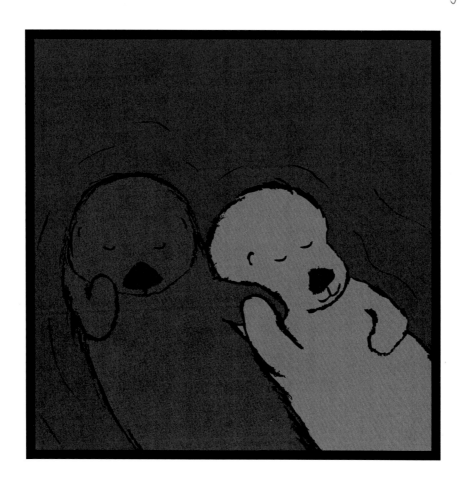

To my loving mom,
Thank you for your continuous support and
for loving these otters as much as I do.

ISBN-13: 978-1-50-875045-1
ISBN-10: 1-508-75045-9
Library of Congress Control Number: 2015904312
CreateSpace Independent Publishing Platform, North Charleston, SC

Close at Heart

A Sea Otter Story

Written & Illustrated by Jill Turner

Once upon a time,
There lived two happy sea otters.
They spent fun-filled days
Playing in California waters.

They basked in the sun
And played with kelp all day.
But when nighttime came,
They found one place to stay.

They slept in the kelp bay,
Which was right where they belong.
They gently closed their eyes
And listened to the waves' calm song.

Then one night something happened
That never happened before.
The waves became stronger
And washed one otter far from shore.

The water began to drift
The otter farther away.
He was now away from his friend
And from the kelp bay.

When the sun began to rise,
He quickly awoke with a fright.
It was then that he noticed
He had drifted away overnight.

He felt so scared and alone.
He missed the other otter so.
He cried out to his good friend.
What to do? He did not know.

A pelican heard his cry
And quickly offered to help.
So she gave the otter directions
Back to the bay of kelp.

The otter thanked the kind pelican
And followed the directions around the bend.
He swam with a determined mind
To find his otter friend.

After a long swim of adventure
Through the cold California water,
He finally came across
His friend - the other otter.

The two otters hugged and hugged.
They had missed each other so!
How could they prevent another parting?
They did not yet know.

So how would they do this?
The two otters thought for a while.
Ah - they came upon a solution,
Which made them both smile.

At night they will hold hands
So they will not drift apart.
They will stay close in distance
And they will stay close at heart.

The End

Made in the USA
San Bernardino, CA
28 September 2016